EGMONT
We bring stories to life

First published in Great Britain in 2018 by Egmont UK Limited,
The Yellow Building, 1 Nicholas Road, London W11 4AN

Content written and adapted by Catherine Shoolbred
Designed by Jeannette O'Toole

© 2018 Disney Enterprises, Inc.

ISBN 978 1 4052 9120 0
68614/001
Printed in EU

This
Frozen Annual
belongs to:

....

Write your name here

From the movie

Disney

FROZEN

ANNUAL 2019

Contents

Meet Elsa 8

Forest Maze 9

Meet Anna 10

Colour Anna 11

Marbles Fun 12

Meet Kristoff and Sven 14

Dot-to-dot Friends 15

Meet Olaf 16

Frozen Names 17

STORY: Olaf's Frozen
Adventure 18

Festive Kiss 24

Mountain Maze 25

STORY: A Huge Help 26

Great Sculptures 28

Dance Cube 29

STORY: Flood Danger 31

On the Beach 37

Carrots on Ice 38

Special Places 40

Ice in Spring 42

STORY: Kristoff's Speech 44

Magical Friends Sudoku 46

Shadow Match 47

STORY: Little Explorers 48

Blooming Hills 54

Rescue Mission 56

Hide-and-Seek 58

Summer Music 60

Magical Moments 62

Posters 63

Goodbye! 67

Answers 68

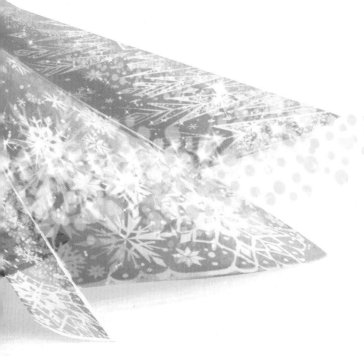

Meet Elsa

Elsa can magically control ICE and SNOW.

When she was younger, she had to hide her POWERS from everyone including her sister, ANNA.

She becomes QUEEN of Arendelle when her parents are lost at sea.

Anna's act of TRUE LOVE teaches Elsa how to control her powers.

Forest Maze

Elsa challenged Olaf to find his way through the forest maze to the tallest tree in the forest. Can you help him get there?

Answers on page 68

Meet Anna

Anna is **ELSA'S** younger sister.

She grows close to **KRISTOFF**, who helps to find her sister on the North Mountain.

Anna agrees to **MARRY** Prince Hans the day she meets him, but later she realises he doesn't love her.

When Elsa's **POWERS** are revealed, Anna follows her to the **NORTH MOUNTAIN** to ask her to stop Arendelle's eternal **WINTER**.

Colour Anna

Add colour to complete
this picture of Anna.

Marbles Fun

The path leading to Arendelle castle is the perfect place for a game of marbles! Join Anna and the village kids for some fun and spot the 12 differences between the two scenes. Colour in the bags as you go!

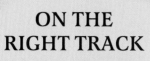

ON THE RIGHT TRACK

Discover the path from the green marble to the red one!

COLOURFUL SEQUENCES

Complete each row by connecting the missing marbles.

Meet Kristoff and Sven

Kristoff is an ICE HARVESTER.

He goes everywhere with his loyal reindeer, SVEN.

Kristoff is brought up by TROLLS.

Sven loves having ADVENTURES with Kristoff.

Kristoff becomes GREAT FRIENDS with Anna, Elsa and Olaf.

Dot-to-dot Friends

Join the dots on Kristoff, then colour in the picture of him with Sven.

8

9 7

10 6

11 5

12 4

13 3

14 2

15 1

25 44 45

24 26

27

16 23 43

22

17 28

20 21

29

19 41 42

18 30

31 40

32 39

33

34

35 38

36 37

Meet Olaf

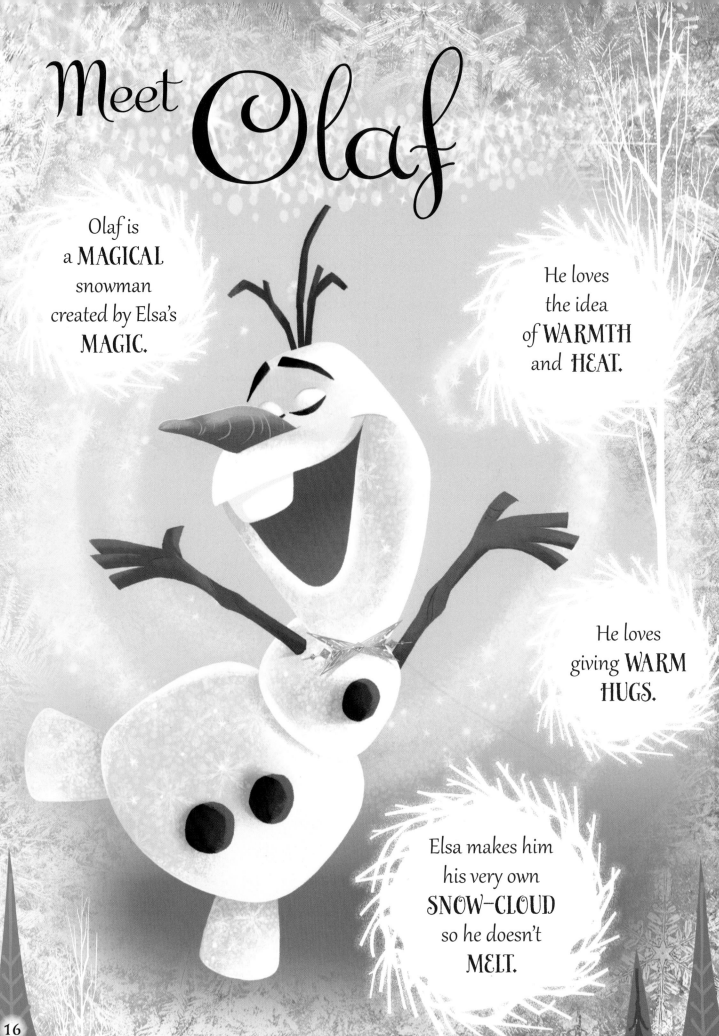

Olaf is a **MAGICAL** snowman created by Elsa's **MAGIC**.

He loves the idea of **WARMTH** and **HEAT**.

He loves giving **WARM HUGS**.

Elsa makes him his very own **SNOW-CLOUD** so he doesn't **MELT**.

16

Frozen Names

Draw lines to add the missing letters
to complete the four names.

O	L		F	N
A	N	A		V
S		E	N	E
	L	S	A	A

Answers on page 68

Olaf's FROZEN ADVENTURE

2 Olaf and Kristoff help decorate the courtyard before the townspeople arrive wearing their best festive clothes.

1 It's Arendelle's first holiday season in forever and Anna and Elsa have organised a party.

3 Then Kristoff and Sven deliver the Yule Bell. "It signals the start of the holidays!" Elsa tells Olaf.

4 Bong! Bong! goes the bell and everyone cheers. Anna and Elsa invite the townspeople to their party, but they all start to leave.

5 When Anna asks why they are going, the people explain they have their own holiday traditions to get back to.

6 They tell her about their different traditions, from baking and candy-making to knitting socks and more.

7 Anna and Elsa realise they're the only ones without a holiday tradition. They are sad to realise that they have missed out on so much.

8 Olaf rushes to tell Sven. "Let's find the best traditions for Anna and Elsa!" he shouts. They immediately set off together.

9 First, Olaf asks a family about their festive tradition of making colourful candy canes.

10 Olaf thinks a candy cane makes a very festive, but rather too sweet nose!

11 He learns about other holiday traditions, from singing and making wreaths to knitting and candle-making.

12 Olaf puts a sample of each tradition, including the Oaken family's portable sauna, on Sven's sleigh to show to Anna and Elsa.

13 But suddenly hot coals from the portable sauna set the sleigh on fire and the traditions all burn!

14 The burning sleigh falls over a cliff, leaving Sven on one side and Olaf on the other side of a ravine.

15 Sven looks at Olaf in horror. The holiday traditions are gone!

16 Olaf has saved one, a fruitcake, which he can show to Anna and Elsa. But then Sven hears wolves growling in the forest ...

17 At the castle, Anna and Elsa look for family traditions in the attic. Anna spots some festive gloves and then she finds a special box.

18 Meanwhile, Sven rushes to the castle to get help for Olaf. He acts like Olaf so Kristoff, Anna and Elsa realise Olaf is in danger due to hungry wolves.

19 As they head into the forest, they spot Olaf's nose sticking out of a snowdrift. He had fought off the wolves but lost the cake – a bird ate it!

20 Anna shows Olaf the box she has found, which is filled with pictures of Olaf that the sisters had drawn when they were little.

21 "You're our holiday tradition, Olaf! All those years when we were alone, you reminded us how much we loved each other!" they tell him.

22 Elsa throws a party to celebrate right there in the forest. She and Anna are thrilled to have rediscovered their own holiday tradition and everyone loves Arendelle's new tradition - a festive forest party inspired by Olaf!

The End

Festive Kiss

A little girl gives Olaf a kiss! Match the jigsaw pieces
to the spaces in the big picture.

Answers on page 68

Mountain Maze

Olaf is determined to find the best holiday traditions for Anna and Elsa. Help him through the maze to the traditions.

Answers on page 68

A Huge Help

Manuscript: Tea Orsi; Layout: Alberto Zanon; Cleanup: Caterina Giorgetti; Colour: MichelAngela World

ELSA AND HER FRIENDS HAVE JUST VISITED THE ICE PALACE ...

FASTER, SVEN!

THERE'S A BIG BUNCH OF CARROTS WAITING FOR YOU AT THE CASTLE!

WOOSH

AND HOT CHOCOLATE FOR THE REST OF US!

HUH? DID YOU HEAR THAT?

HOOOOO

IT COMES FROM THAT SLEDGE!

IT SOUNDS LIKE AN ANIMAL IN DANGER!

HOOOOO

AND ...

IT'S A SLED DOG! HOW DID HE END UP DOWN THERE?

I DON'T KNOW BUT WE HAVE TO RESCUE HIM!

HELLO-O-O! I CAN'T WAIT TO GIVE YOU A WARM HUG!

The End

27

Great Sculptures

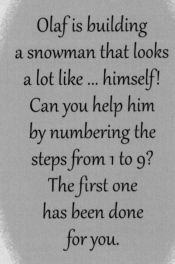

Olaf is building a snowman that looks a lot like ... himself! Can you help him by numbering the steps from 1 to 9? The first one has been done for you.

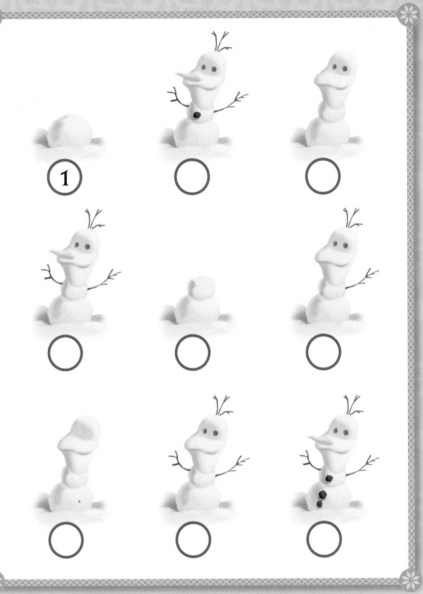

Draw over the dotted letters to name Elsa and Anna's magical snowman friend.

Answers on page 68

Dance Cube

Make this Frozen dance cube and get ready to dance!

1 Carefully cut along the dashed lines.

2 Fold along the white lines and stick the tabs down with glue to make the cube.

3 Roll the dice and dance!

Stick

Jump

Stick

1 arm up

Stick

Stick

© Disney

Spin

Stick

Wave

2 arms up
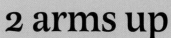

Stick

Hop

Stick

Stick

Ask a grown-up to help.

29

Flood Danger

OUR FRIENDS ARE GETTING BACK AFTER A LONG HIKE ON THE MOUNTAINS ...

WHAT A GREAT HIKE!

YOU'RE RIGHT, ANNA!

IT WOULD HAVE BEEN EVEN BETTER IF IT HADN'T **RAINED** ALL THE TIME!

BUT NOW WE ARE REALLY CLOSE TO ARENDELLE!

YES, WE ARE HERE!

GREAT! AND HOPEFULLY IT WON'T RAIN UNTIL WE GET HOME!

?!?

ERM ...

PLOP

MAYBE IT WAS **JUST** A DROP ...

SLURP

Manuscript: Tea Orsi; Layout: Alberto Zanon; Cleanup: Letizia Algeri; Colour: MichelAngela World

WOOOSH

NO! IT WASN'T!

I'M AFRAID OUR HIKE IS OVER!

OH NO!

LET'S FIND SOME SHELTER!

QUICK!

LUCKILY ...

LOOK! THERE'S A HOUSE OVER THERE!

LET'S GO AND ASK IF WE CAN GO IN!

SO ...

KNOCK KNOCK

AND ...

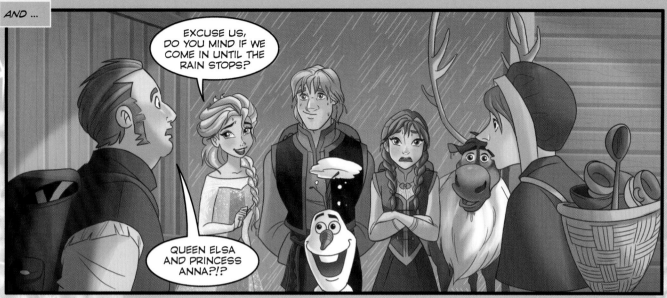

EXCUSE US, DO YOU MIND IF WE COME IN UNTIL THE RAIN STOPS?

QUEEN ELSA AND PRINCESS ANNA?!?

OH, I'VE NEVER BEEN HUGGED BY A SNOWMAN!

MY NAME IS OLAF AND I LIKE WARM HUGS!

ARE YOU GETTING READY FOR A JOURNEY?

KIND OF, PRINCESS ANNA! I'M AFRAID WE ALL SHOULD LEAVE SOON!

LEAVE?!? WHY?

THE RIVER MIGHT OVERFLOW ANY MINUTE NOW! STAYING HERE IS NOT SAFE!

WE BUILT BARRIERS, BUT IT HAS BEEN RAINING TOO MUCH!

THE WATER LEVEL IS RISING BY THE MINUTE!

STAYING HERE IS TOO DANGEROUS FOR YOU!

WHY DON'T WE TRY TO BUILD HIGHER BARRIERS?

THE RAIN IS TOO HEAVY! WE WON'T BE ABLE TO WORK OUTSIDE!

WHAT CAN WE DO? THE WATER WILL FLOOD OUR HOUSE AND OUR FIELDS!

LET'S CHECK THE WATER LEVEL!

YEAH, THERE'S NO TIME TO WASTE!

THANK YOU, QUEEN ELSA!

YOU SAVED OUR HOUSE!

AND IT'S FINALLY STOPPED RAINING! WE CAN GO OUT.

ARE WE GOING TO ICE-SKATE ON THE RIVER?

NO, OLAF! I HAVE ANOTHER IDEA.

AND ...

WHEN I'M DONE I WILL TAKE THE ICE TO THE MOUNTAINS!

SO IT WON'T BE DANGEROUS WHEN IT MELTS!

PICK PICK

GOOD JOB, ELSA!

I COULDN'T HAVE DONE IT WITHOUT YOU! WE'RE THE BEST TEAM EVER!

The End

On the Beach

Anna hurries to catch up with Elsa and Olaf, but the water's ice-cold! Take her by the hand and help her wade through the maze to the boat!

Carrots on Ice

Elsa's having a ball with Sven! She's left some carrots along the path that the reindeer needs to follow to catch up with Olaf.

Play this board game with your friends. Put coins or counters by Sven, then take turns rolling the dice and follow the instructions (see top right) about the special spaces you may land on. The first to the finish wins!

START

1 2 3 4 5 6 7 8 9 10 11 12 13 14 15 16 17

SPECIAL SPACES:

Run to catch a sliding carrot: ADVANCE 3 SPACES.

Sven grabs a carrot before it sinks in the snow: ADVANCE 4 SPACES.

Want a snack? Start digging! GO BACK 1 SPACE.

Great carrot! This snowman looks like Olaf ... Go! ADVANCE 2 SPACES.

Sven will have to wait till the ice melts: LOSE 1 TURN.

FINISH

38

37

36

35

34

33

32

31

30

29

28

27

26

25

24

23

22

21

20

19

18

39

Special Places

There's plenty to do in Arendelle, and Elsa's about to enjoy a fabulous day around town, meeting some very interesting people. To start, colour in the portrait the royal artist has drawn of her.

ALLURING FRAGRANCES

Sweet scents fill the air! Follow the paths to put the letters in the right order and find out what Elsa is going to buy.

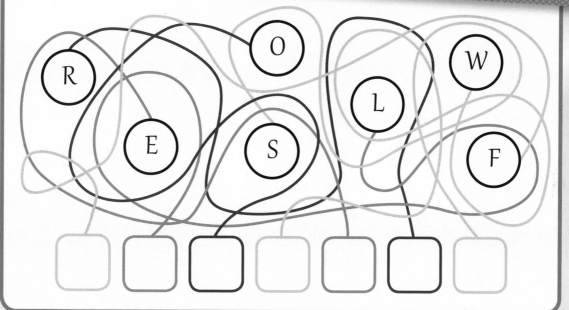

A PRECIOUS TOUCH

In the end, Elsa goes to a special shop to buy a present for Anna. Match up the pairs of objects. The one left over is what she buys.

Answers on page 69

Ice in Spring

Elsa has frozen the pond so Anna and her friends can do some ice-skating while enjoying the warmth of spring.

Spot the 12 differences in these two scenes, and colour in the skates as you go.

MAGIC SOLUTION

And when a storm hits ... Elsa creates an elegant ice shelter.
Connect the missing pieces to complete these two scenes.
Look out for the odd-ones-out!

Kristoff's Speech

Manuscript: Alessandro Ferrari; Layout: Alberto Zanon; Cleanup: Veronica Di Lorenzo; Colour: Dario Calabria

"THIRD, YOU'LL MEET SOME TONGUE TWISTER EXPERTS ..."

THREE THRUMMING THIRSTY THIEVES THRUSTING THREE THRONES THROUGH A THRIVING OF THORNS!

I FORBEAR, BUT I CAN'T BEAR TO HEAR WITH A BEAR IN MY EAR THIS YEAR!

"FINALLY YOU'LL BE READY FOR YOUR SPEECH!"

I HOPE I CAN. I MEAN, I **KNOW** I CAN. THANK YOU, ANNA.

REMEMBER ... EVERY WORD COUNTS! AND DON'T FORGET TO BREATHE!

HONOURED GUESTS ...

... WELCOME TO ARENDELLE!

YEAH!

GOOD JOB KRISTOFF!

CLAP CLAP CLAP

YOU'RE THE BEST!

WAIT, THAT WAS YOUR SPEECH ... FIVE WORDS?

I KNOW, BUT EVERY WORD COUNTS.

The End

45

Magical Friends Sudoku

Elsa has brought the snowgies outside the Ice Palace to play ... but they're out of control! See if you can keep them in order.

Complete the grid by connecting the missing characters. Each row and column must contain 4 different snowgies.

Answers on page 69

Shadow Match

Draw lines to match up our favourite friends with their shadows.

1

2

A

B

C

D

3

4

Answers on page 69

Little Explorers

Manuscript: Tea Orsi; Layout: Alberto Zanon; Cleanup: Letizia Algeri; Colour: Dario Calabria

ANNA HAS A COLD ...

OH, I REALLY WANTED TO GO OUT TODA-A-A-AATCHOO!

COME ON, ANNA! YOU'LL BE BETTER SOON!

I KNOW! SNIFF ... BUT THIS IS SO BORING ...

LET'S SEE IF THIS WILL MAKE YOU CHANGE YOUR MIND!

GASP! THAT WAS ONE OF OUR FAVOURITE BOOKS!

I KNEW YOU WOULD REMEMBER IT!

OF COURSE I DO! IT'S THE STORY OF THE TWO KIDS WHO GOT LOST AND ...

LIVED A FANTASTIC ADVENTURE IN AN UNEXPLORED LAND!

WHAT IS AN UNEXPLORED LAND, ANNA?

OH, HI, OLAF!

IT'S A NEW PLACE THAT NO ONE HAS GOT TO KNOW YET.

REALLY?!? TELL ME MORE ABOUT THIS STORY!

ATCHOO!

WE'LL READ IT TOGETHER!

YES, WHEN WE WERE LITTLE WE LOVED IT SO MUCH THAT ONCE WE TRIED TO ACT IT OUT!

"IT WAS A SUNNY AFTERNOON AND OUR MOTHER WAS READING THE BOOK OUT LOUD FOR US ..."

SO THE KIDS FOUND THEIR WAY HOME, AND THEY LOOKED FORWARD TO TELLING EVERYONE ABOUT ...

... THEIR AMAZING ADVENTURE!

"AND AFTER THE STORY, WE COULDN'T WAIT TO PLAY ..."

WE'RE GOING TO EXPLORE THE WOODS, MOTHER!

DON'T GO TOO FAR, GIRLS!

LET'S GO, ELSA! I WANT TO FIND A NEW LAND, LIKE THE KIDS IN THE BOOK!

GOOD IDEA, ANNA!

WOW! DID YOU FIND THE UNKNOWN LAND?

WELL, WE PRETENDED IT WAS IN THE WOODS!

WE DIDN'T KNOW IT THAT WELL, SO IT WAS KIND OF UNEXPLORED FOR US!

"SO WE STARTED LOOKING AROUND ..."

THESE MUST BE YUMMYLICIOUS BERRIES ...

HMMM ... THEY DON'T LOOK LIKE THE ONES IN THE BOOK. WHAT IF YOU CAN'T EAT THEM?

IT'S NOT FAIR! IN THE BOOK ALL THE BERRIES WERE DELICIOUS!

BUT THEY CLIMBED THE HIGH MOUNTAIN AND SAW THEIR HOME FROM UP THERE!

THERE IS NO MOUNTAIN HERE, ANNA ...

WAIT A MINUTE, MAYBE ...

I CAN TRY TO MAKE IT!

YOU'RE RIGHT. DO THE MAGIC, ELSA!

WHAT DID YOU MAKE ELSA?

IT WAS ...

"... SOMETHING THAT LOOKED LIKE A MOUNTAIN ..."

LOOK! THEY ARE DOWN THERE!

I CAN'T BELIEVE IT!

"IT TURNED OUT THAT OUR UNEXPLORED LAND WAS JUST A FEW STEPS AWAY FROM OUR PARENTS."

MAYBE WE WERE NOT SO LOST AS WE THOUGHT!

NOW, LET'S READ THE ORIGINAL STORY!

I THINK I'M FEELING MUCH BETTER!

LET'S PLAN A NEW ADVENTURE FOR TOMORROW!

CAN I COME TOO?

SURE!

AAAAATCHOOOOO!

WELL, MAYBE WE'LL GO THE DAY AFTER TOMORROW!

The End

Blooming Hills

There are lots of great places around Arendelle to enjoy a summer walk. Today our friends have brought along a picnic for their relaxing stroll. Join them and colour in Sven!

WHAT'S FOR LUNCH?

Connect the dots from 1 to 23 to reveal an object our friends use to carry their food.

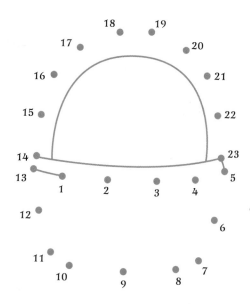

NATURE GIFT
Follow the dots to colour in the pretty rose!

NATURAL SCENTS
Draw the missing parts of the bouquets and colour them in like the example. Then complete the series by drawing and colouring the last one.

Rescue Mission

Anna and Elsa love exploring the Arendelle countryside. Today they've found a reindeer calf in need of help. Follow and colour the pairs of hoofprints that lead to the reindeer and then colour him in too!

START

A COLOURFUL FRIEND
*Draw your very own butterfly
then colour it in.*

FINISH

Answers on page 69

Hide-and-Seek

Olaf loves playing with the baby trolls. Today those rascals are hiding all over the place! Join the fun and help him find them: Circle each one you spot and tick them off in the purple circles below as you go!

MORE PLAYERS

Kristoff and Sven are taking a break. Enjoy a little rest with them and write the numbers in the blanks to rearrange the jumbled picture.

TO RUN EVERYWHERE IS ...

... THEIR FAVOURITE SPORT!

BULDA'S SENTENCE

- What is she saying about the baby trolls? Hold up a mirror to read her second speech bubble. Then write the words below.

... T _ _ _ _ _

_ _ _ _ _ _ _ _ _ _ _ _ _ _!

Answers on page 69

Summer Music

On this beautiful day, Kristoff treats Anna, Elsa and Olaf to a song! Find the path from Kristoff to each friend, then count the notes and write the numbers in the circles.

Anna = ○ Elsa = ○ Olaf = ○

SWEET MELODY

What's the title of Kristoff's lovely tune? To find out, write the letters you see under the symbols in the boxes on the right.

❄	▲	❋
D	E	F
◆	✿	●
G	I	N
✳	◎	☆
O	R	S

Answers on page 69

61

Magical Moments

Here are three happy memories of little sisters at play! Complete the pictures by writing the letters of each missing piece next to the matching pieces below.

A

B

1 ☐ 2 ☐

3 ☐ 4 ☐

5 ☐ 6 ☐

C

Answers on page 69

From the movie

Disney

FROZEN

SISTERS FOREVER

From the movie

Disney

From the movie

Disney
FROZEN

Warm
HUGS
all round!

© 2018 Disney

CUT ALONG HERE